Finding Grandma's Memories

by Jiyeon Pak

ALFRED A. KNOPF · NEW YORK

Ever since I was really little, I have loved having tea with my grandma.

She lets me choose my own teacup from her treasure shelf.

And she always adds the perfect amount of honey and milk.

"Berry milk tea and chocolate cupcakes are my favorite!"

"This berry milk tea recipe came from *my* grandma. It's a very old recipe."

During teatime, I tell
Grandma about my day.

And Grandma tells me stories
from when she was a little girl.

But as I got bigger, teatime started to change.

Once, Grandma got my name confused.

Another time she forgot to turn off the water while filling the kettle.

She accidentally put her teacup on the bookshelf instead of on her treasure shelf.

And she left her eyeglasses in the refrigerator.

My parents told me that Grandma was losing her memory. That meant she could forget things, even things she used to know well.

I felt worried.
I wanted to find
a way to help her!

The next time we had tea, Grandma brought out her photo album.

Inside were photos of the people from Grandma's stories.

There was a photo from her wedding.

A photo of Grandma and a cute dog.

There was even a photo of Grandma with a little girl who had hair just like mine!

Grandma turned the photo over and read the note on the back, "Me and Mary."

Then she told me a story about her best friend, Mary, and all the fun they had.

Aha! *That's who Mary was!*

Grandma's photos
gave me an idea.

With Grandma's help, we put notes around her house to remind her where things go and what to do.

I even made Grandma
a can't-lose-them chain
for her eyeglasses!

Sometimes,
Grandma still forgets
to turn off the water

or can't find
her keys.

And her teacups are still
left in strange places.

I hope Grandma will always remember our teatime. But it's okay if she forgets. Because I can remind her about *our* stories.

*To those who remain
precious in our memories*

THIS IS A BORZOI BOOK PUBLISHED BY ALFRED A. KNOPF

Copyright © 2019 by Jiyeon Pak

All rights reserved. Published in the United States by Alfred A. Knopf,
an imprint of Random House Children's Books,
a division of Penguin Random House LLC, New York.

Knopf, Borzoi Books, and the colophon are registered trademarks
of Penguin Random House LLC.

Visit us on the Web! rhcbooks.com

Educators and librarians, for a variety of teaching tools, visit us at RHTeachersLibrarians.com

Library of Congress Cataloging-in-Publication Data is available upon request.

ISBN 978-0-525-58107-9 (trade) — ISBN 978-0-525-58108-6 (lib. bdg.) —
ISBN 978-0-525-58109-3 (ebook)

The text of this book is set in 22-point Brandon Grotesque.

The illustrations were created with acrylic paints and colored pencils, then collaged digitally.

Book design by Jinna Shin

MANUFACTURED IN CHINA

September 2019

10 9 8 7 6 5 4 3 2 1

First Edition